Widowed Sloane Whittman never expects to find love again, but it happens when she meets up with Seth again—the man her dead husband and everyone else on Cape Cod call Joe. Christmas is coming, and Sloane is all for giving her son his Christmas wish for a new dad. The solution seems clear, marry Seth, but several glitches throw a monkey wrench into her plans.

Seth is madly in love with Sloane but worries she might feel he's less than a man because of his life-changing injuries from a shark attack. His sister is in a coma, and his niece Janie is wishing for her mom to wake up for Christmas. He can only pray for a Christmas miracle.

Will everyone get their Christmas Miracle? Or will the Grinch steal their dreams?

Cape Cod Christmas
Copyright © 2024 Kathy Kalmar
ISBN: 978-1-4874-4258-3
Cover art by Martine Jardine

Published by eXtasy Books Inc

Look for us online at:
www.eXtasybooks.com

Cape Cod Christmas
Cape Cod 3

By

Kathy Kalmar

DEDICATION

To Larry, who gave me my very own second chance to love, more happiness than I could have believed possible, and healed three broken hearts in the process. I swear I can't love you any more than I already do and the next day proves me wrong. It takes a special man to mend hearts he didn't break and children he didn't make. You do that, my love. And you make our Christmases very merry and bright.

In Memoriam
With love
To my forever friend, Linda Wilson, whose skills, talents, and belief in me and my work led to this publication and every book I write. Ours is a relationship forged in the fires of pain, loss, love, and laughter. Living without you is very difficult. You'd love this one!
To Ron Wilson, my best bud, whose deep and abiding friendship led me to Cape Cod.

Acknowledgment

For Carolyn Gilbreath. Her counsel and encouragement made this a better book. She is my Best Friend Forever. And with great gratitude, I acknowledge Tina Haveman for her great vision and company, Jay Austin, extraordinary Editor in Chief; Debbie Nygaard, editor, and wise counsel; Martine Jardin, artist; Bri Vries, assistant to the Editor in Chief, The Greater Detroit Romance Writers; Ron and Ginger Wilson who took us all over Cape Cod and introduced us to our special place; Jane Campo, for telling me to keep Cape Cod in the title and you, my readers.
Lastly, Doug Marple, the webmaster, who keeps the social media site wheels turning. I'm grateful to you all.

CHAPTER ONE: WISHES

Sunday Before Christmas

Janie glanced out her window, watching the snow fall softly on the boardwalk around her home—the Sail Inn in Truro, Cape Cod. Christmas fairy lights covered the arch trellis that led to the oyster shell parking lot, and the falling snow made the lights twinkle like fireflies in the summer beach grass. They were going to church any minute, so she had to hurry to write her letter to Santa. She decided to mail it from St. Joan of Arc Catholic Church. Surely the church could beat the post office any day and speed it on its way because she was in a hurry.

Since she just got the idea when she woke up, she had to do it now. She tore a page out of her school notebook and began writing as fast as she could. She had to cross out several mistakes and hoped Santa and God wouldn't mind.

Dear Santa,

I wanna ask you for two things for Christmas. First, will you use your magic and wake Mom up for Christmas, pretty please, with sugar on top. She's in a coma and has been sleeping for months, but you already know that. Sorry for reminding you. Second, can you share this letter with God? You might need his help to wake Mom. Can you also tell God to say Hi to my daddy while you're at it? He went to heaven last spring, and I miss him soooo much. Well, I guess that's it. That's all I want for Christmas. Forever. I promise. Cross my heart and hope to die. Please, she's the bestest Mom ever, and I need her!

Love,
Your friend,
Jane Marie Davies

The next she knew, her Uncle Joe was telling her to shake a leg, or they'd be late for Mass. She folded her note, stuck it in an envelope, and wrote *To Santa Clause* on the outside.

The ride to St. Joan of Arc Catholic Church took longer because of the snow, but Janie didn't mind. It was pretty outside, and the snow was sticking, which was a good thing because Santa could use his sleigh and magic reindeer to take her letter straight to heaven.

The streetlights sparkled with the lacey snowflake decorations that hung from them. Uncle Joe put the radio on, and Silent Night was playing. It made her feel warm and happy. She just knew her idea to write to Santa and God had to do the trick to wake her mom up in time for Christmas.

When they arrived at the clapboard church, Janie stopped at Saint Joan's statue next to the Nativity display. Garlands decorated Saint Joan, and a big red felt bow rested on her shoulder. Janie knew St. Joan was a warrior for God, so she asked her to join her mom's battle to wake up.

She heard the organ playing O Come All Ye Faithful as she entered the church. She quickly pushed her missive through the slot in the box next to the votive candles folks lit to lift their prayers to heaven. She supposed since heat rises — she learned that in science class — the candle smoke would carry her Christmas letter straight to heaven. *That oughta do it.*

Janie walked down the aisle to join her uncle and forgot to genuflect when she saw Joel and Miss Sloane. She nearly forgot they were coming back to have a Cape Cod Christmas. They'd flown to Michigan with Addie to take care of . . . something. She wasn't sure what, but she was happy they were back.

She quickly sent a Snapchat to Joel.

u write your letter?
He responded with a thumbs up.
Sick. U ask for a family for Christmas?
Another thumbs up showed in her feed, followed by a text.
Dad died and broke the fam. I asked God for a new one.
Sick.

Joel scowled when Miss Sloan threw him the side eye and confiscated his phone.

Janie quickly pocketed her phone and slipped into the pew next to her uncle just as the bells rang, signaling the beginning of Mass. She glanced around at all the decorations the church had put up. The beamed ceiling was festooned with fragrant evergreen garlands, and several real trees were strategically placed throughout the church and clustered around another Nativity set. Faux candles and red bows were tied to the aisle end of each pew. The low church lights and twinkling fairy lights created a joyous vibe.

The sermon celebrated Gaudete Sunday, the third Sunday of Advent. Janie had learned that Gaudete means rejoice because the Lord will come soon. Joy filled the church with excitement, expectation, and warmth, giving Janie hope. On that note, she hoped Joel had mailed his letter to Santa and God like they had discussed in earlier conversations. But he was a guy, so she didn't know if he followed the plan.

Like her, Joel was a half-orphan, too. Joel's dad had died during the pandemic, and Joel missed him a whole lot. More than anything, he frequently talked about how he wanted to be a *real* family again. He felt he only had half a family since it was just him and his mom.

Janie figured she had less of a family since her dad died due to an IED explosion, and her mom, a war correspondent, was seriously injured in the same event. That made her wonder. *Am I a full orphan? Or a half orphan?*

The church choir sang Angels We Have Heard on High, and she let her heart swell with hope again. *Aunt Monalisa always tells me to think positive.*

Aunt Monalisa had stayed home, still recovering from a heart attack brought on by a fall into the ocean. Even worse, a shark bit into her Uncle Joe's leg when he rescued Aunt Monalisa. She knew it hurt him like the dickens—whatever that meant—and he hadn't been the same since.

Janie prayed that Miss Sloane could bring Uncle Joe back to himself again. *This family sure needs a Christmas miracle, God.* She took a chance to glance at Joel. His eyes were closed, and he looked serious. *Is he praying for his family, too?*

The bells chimed. The priest raised the Host, then the cup, signaling the holiest time in the Mass. She knew in her heart that this was the best time to ask God for a big favor. She snuck a look at Miss Sloane and Uncle Joe. They too had their heads bent, their expressions fervent. She bet they were all praying for the same thing.

"Merry Almost Christmas, God," she whispered. "Thanks for bringing Miss Sloane and Joel home for Christmas."

After Mass, Janie, Joel, Miss Sloane, and Uncle Joe gathered together. Uncle Joe walked with a limp, but that didn't affect his upper body strength. He lifted Miss Sloane off her feet and whirled her around like they did in the movies. Several parishioners applauded when Uncle Joe kissed Miss Sloane. Janie and Joel giggled and launched into their k-i-s-s-i-n-g refrain.

Miss Sloane laughed, and color flooded her cheeks. "Put me down, sailor, we're attracting a crowd." She made a playful curtsy and then made a beeline for her car in the parking lot.

"Follow me," Seth called over his shoulder to her retreating back. "We're all staying at Monalisa's."

"Just text me her address. This car has GPS."

He chuckled.

Aunt Monalisa owned a house located behind her gallery in Wellfleet, where they all stayed during the months Sail Inn was closed for the season. The Inn had heat, but the harsh Atlantic winters sent them inland to avoid some of the penetrating winds of Truro.

Due to Aunt Monalisa's physical therapy and health issues, Janie knew she'd waited for Sloane and Joel to arrive to decorate the house. After the drive from church, their *almost* family gathered amid greetings, hugs, and luggage in the living room. Later in the day, Aunt Monalisa would most likely accompany them to Fair Haven Rehabilitation Center to decorate her mom's nursing home room. First, everyone focused on getting Miss Sloane and Joel settled in.

After everyone feasted on Monalisa's succulent roast dinner, Miss Sloane pulled Uncle Joe aside, but Janie was close enough to hear her.

"I think Joel has had enough for one day. Do you mind if we stay home tonight?" Miss Sloane said.

Janie glanced at Joel and watched him rub his eyes and yawn.

"I'm getting dream crumbs in my eyes," Joel grumbled. "Where's my PJs, Mom?"

Janie's jaw nearly cracked when she caught Joel's contagious yawn. Yeah, she was tired, too.

Uncle Joe chuckled. "No problem. Janie's had a full day, too. Tomorrow's another day. We'll go see Mal then."

CHAPTER TWO: THE CALL

Monday Before Christmas

Seth's phone chimed as they sat around the breakfast table. He frowned when he saw the caller ID and answered. After a brief greeting and explanation, he said, "I see. We'll be there as soon as we can."

Sloane threw him a quick look, and he palmed the back of his neck, feeling agitated but struggling not to alarm the children. He knew trouble brewed when the caller greeted him as *Mr. Bradford*.

He sighed, then straightened his shoulders to say, "Change of plans." He cleared his throat and looked at Sloane. "Would you come with me for a couple of hours?" He stood from his chair, silently cursing the pain gripping his leg and heart. "Monalisa, can you keep these scalawags busy while I deal with Fair Haven?"

Janie perked up. "Can me and Joel go, too? I made decorations for Mom's room. Miss Sloane and Joel can help us."

Seth hesitated. "It's a business meeting." He glanced outside. "Maybe later on. The weather doesn't look that great, but let me take care of things, then we'll talk about the rest." He darted a look at Monalisa.

Monalisa caught on and smiled. "It's Joel and Miss Sloane's first Christmas on Cape Cod. Let's make it magical." She snapped her fingers. "I know what we should do. I planned to make special sea ornaments. I need you and Joel to help me. Why don't we do that now?"

Joel squealed. "Fresh!"

Monalisa ushered the children through the French doors to her home art studio, where she had an assortment of driftwood, sea stars, sand dollars, ribbons, sea glass, and glitter to aid their creativity.

Seth helped Sloane with her parka as they said their goodbyes. He helped her navigate through the strong sea breeze to his *Jeep*.

Sloane shivered as he helped into the passenger seat. "Brr. While I love the summer Tradewinds, this is a bit too icy." She huddled into her jacket and raised its hood to block the cold.

Seth got behind the wheel. "I'm dreading this conversation. Something's brewing, I can feel it, and it's not good." He couldn't help the worry and tension that filled his tone.

Sloane placed her hand on his thigh, probably hoping to offer him comfort because no words would counter the dread and sorrow he felt in his gut. Platitudes wouldn't cut it.

Seth drove carefully through the falling sleet with the four-wheel drive engaged. The roads, with their twists and curves, were icing up. The *Jeep* skidded, and he decreased his speed even more.

The drive to Provincetown normally took just over thirty minutes in good traffic and weather, but with the deteriorating conditions, the trip took over an hour. *Why call us out into this weather? It must be serious.* Seth tensed up with worry, fear, and not a little concern as he parked as close as possible to the sprawling one-story Fair Haven Rehab Center. The fierce winds almost tore the car door from his hand when he opened it and nearly wrested the door to the Center off its hinges, only to have it shut with a loud slam once they were blown inside.

Rene de Groupe, the facility's director, met them in the cozy lobby and quietly ushered them down the wide hall past the crackling fire and into her office. The bay window permitted a turbulent contrast to the serenity of her office but mirrored his feelings perfectly.

Rene invited them to sit and offered tea, no doubt meant to brace, comfort, and soothe them. "Tea on a wintery Cape Cod helps," she suggested as she sat behind the protection of her desk with a look of compassion filling her eyes.

Seth didn't want any damned tea, no matter how bracing or soothing. He cut to the chase. "What's going on? Why did you bring us out in the middle of the storm?"

"Mr. Bradford . . ." she began, her tone firm and business-like as she looked him in the eye for a half second. Although she showed compassion, she had trouble maintaining eye contact.

He stiffened at hearing *Mr. Bradford* again, knowing this was worse than he feared earlier. More serious. More ominous. More consequential. "Has something happened to Mallory?"

"That's the problem. As you know, *nothing* is happening. There's been no change in her condition since she was admitted. Nothing. Has. Changed."

"She's holding her own then?" Seth raised his voice unintentionally—or not—and it reverberated throughout the room. He noticed Sloane and Rene flinch and struggled to regain his control. In a more moderate tone, he ground out, "The doctors said that was a good sign."

Rene held up a hand. "It is. It is. But outside of reflexive motor activity, there's still no sign of—"

"People come out of comas all the time. It hasn't been that long since she arrived. Your organization is designed for coma victims. You're the treatment experts."

"That's why we're so concerned. She still exhibits no reaction to deep pain. Her muscle tone is poor. Her breathing isn't voluntary, and we've seen no progress whatsoever. It's nearly a year since she got here, and frankly, the prognosis is poor, even declining."

"You want her in what, a hospice?" He was half out of his chair and mind when Sloane reached for his hand and pulled him back. "What do you call it? Some sort of do-nothing care? Mere maintenance?"

"Palliative care is the most we can do. I'm sorry."

"What you are saying is pull the plug." He bowed his head, his eyes filling. "Just brushing her off like some random annoying snowflake." He paused for a long moment, then looked her in the eyes. "Tell me, if it was your sister, what would you do?"

Rene winced as if he'd slapped her. "I'd, I'd . . ."

"Exactly. I'm taking her home." He swallowed hard before he spoke again. "It's Christmas. Janie can't lose her mother now. If Mal can hold on, so can we. I'm taking her home."

Rene nodded mutely, pausing, then shook herself as if she had been in deep thought. "I'll send an order to Sea Waters Medical with everything you'll need for her home care. Here's a list of the people we recommend. As soon as we can get things together, we'll make arrangements for her transfer."

Seth stood albeit unsteadily but kept his voice firm. "Right. She's coming home for Christmas."

Chapter Three: Home for the Holidays

Monday Evening

Sloane took the car keys from Seth since he was too upset to drive. She took on the mantle of saviour to get him safely to shore. The weather worsened, making it unsafe to drive any further. Mercifully, she found a hotel near the outskirts of Provincetown that had a room available. She secured a room for the night and led Seth to the bar, ordering him a Scotch double of their best.

She stepped away from the table and called Monalisa, filled her in, and then asked to speak to Joel.

Joel chatted excitedly about the pirate ornament he had made. "It's so cool, Mom, you gotta see it. I used two sand dollars and turned them into a pirate snowman. I made him an eyepatch."

She laughed. "Clever boy." To her surprise, he didn't protest when she told him they'd be home after breakfast the next day.

"Do you think this is a blizzard, Mom? The TV says it's a nor'easter. Think we'll get any candy?" He chuckled. "Get it, Mom? Easter?"

She could help but chuckle, appreciating his humor. Her boy was healing from his selective mutism. Now if only Mal would heal as well.

The hotel's lobby and bar were decorated to the hilt with

garlands, big white bows, candles, lights, and Christmas trees decked in silver, white, and gold. Elegant yet warm. Designed to bring Christmas cheer to travelers.

She found Seth slumped in his chair at the small table near the fire where she'd left him. He appeared shrouded in sorrow, dangerously close to the abyss she had circled herself when they reconnected last summer. She had shouted and screamed at him and into the yawning darkness. She feared the returning echo that could swamp Seth's fragile grief. *Screaming hadn't worked for me. All I got out of it was a sore throat.*

She ordered hot Irish coffees for them both, hoping for a miracle, praying for one, trying to find the right words to comfort Seth. He roused when she brought the drinks over.

"This will cure what ails you," she said. "Where there is life, there is hope. Where there is hope, there is a Christmas miracle."

He gave a weak side smile. "We need several."

"Huh?"

He winced as he shifted his weight, obviously feeling pain in his shark-wounded leg. "Well, I'm hardly savior material anymore. I can't even save my own damn broken half-a-man self, how can I save Mallory?"

"You can't."

"Huh?"

"But I know a guy who can."

"You do?"

"Yes. He's a prayer away."

"What?"

"Wait and see. Believe she'll heal. I do. So can you. You have nothing to lose. Just rely on the magic and mystery of Christmas. You're not the only Savior, mister. Someone else is, and He can do anything. We are going to save Christmas for the kids and save Mallory, too. I don't know how, but somebody I know does. We'll bring Mallory home. Surround her with love, peace, and joy. That will help her. Believe it."

11

"You think so?"

"I do." She raised her hand to her heart." I know. I can feel it."

" I can't take much more, Sloane." He slumped again. "I'm broken. I'm not the same man I used to be. I'm powerless."

"That's bullshit! Man up, buttercup."

His head snapped up. "Who are you calling a buttercup? I'm a snapdragon, to say the least."

She leaned forward, jabbing his chest with her index finger. "Then act like it. You can pray, hope, believe, and help her hang on. You can do plenty, so stop with the pity right now."

He shook his head. "I've had enough. I'm all washed up and worn out."

"You're just tired. It's been a rough day. You have to keep the faith. It's the season for wishes and miracles."

He sighed and gave her a half-smile. "I'll try."

"There is no try. There's do or don't do."

"Who are you? Yoda?"

She tugged him to his feet and hugged him. "Let's go shut this day down." She led him out of the bar and upstairs to their room.

Along the way, she spied a Nativity scene in the lobby and remembered theirs at home. She thought about Joel's letter to Santa tucked away in the manger alongside the infant. She'd debated whether to read it, but in the end, she had not. At the time, she was unsure if she should spirit it away, but she'd been busy packing and shopping for their trip and forgot.

She squeezed Seth's hand. "Here's our room, you'll feel better in the morning."

Since they hadn't planned an overnight trip, Sloane slipped out of her clothes to sleep in her camisole and panties. Seth crawled into bed in his boxer briefs and t-shirt. She yearned to envelop him in her arms, draw him deep inside her, give him a night to remember, and banish his cares, but that would have to wait. Although she knew hot lovemaking after such a long separation would distract him, she also knew he was soul-tired. Instead, she pulled him closer to her. He burrowed into her arms and soon fell asleep. Outside their frosted windowpane, the storm raged.

The next morning, Sloane wanted to make sure Seth would rise to the joy and promise of the new day. She shed her undies and caressed the crest of his ear with her fingers. Keeping her touch feather-light, she stroked the length of his shoulders and played with his firm upper body, toying with his chest hairs and responsive nipples. After a few minutes, he began to stir, and she started her full-body offensive with a series of soft kisses along his jawline while snuggling her bare breasts against him.

Seth moaned and gently pulled her closer. "What's going on?"

"Nothing." She ran her fingers up and down his hard chest. "Just having a hard time with my fingers is all. They keep wanting to do . . ."

Her fingers danced from his nipples to his crotch and played with the elastic of his briefs. She teased his taut body, savoring the feel of his warm skin and occasionally dipping beneath his briefs until she reached his pubic nest and found his rising cock, weeping with his natural lubricant. He reacted by pulling her on top of him until she had no choice but to straddle him. His hands roamed her backside, cupping her cheeks and squeezing them.

Reaching behind her, she fiddled with his sacks until she felt his full hardness beneath her. She raised her hips and guided his hard length inside her needy core. She rode him like a bareback rodeo star as he bucked in sync with her moves. She gave as good as she got, and her climax struck hard and fast.

His thrusts became erratic with his climax, making her inner muscles clench, squeeze, release, and clench again and again until she wrung every last drop from him. Sated, she collapsed on him.

He gently rolled her to the side, kissing her deeply and repeatedly until his smartwatch alarm rang, reminding them of the tasks that awaited them. "I'd like to shower together, but—"

She laughed. "I know. Not enough time."

He shrugged and reluctantly rolled out of reach as he headed to the bathroom shower.

"Run a bath for me when you're done, please. I'm not sure I could go another round after that one."

He looked over his shoulder when he reached the bathroom door and waggled his eyebrows. "Is that a challenge? I bet I could convince you."

I'm sure you could. She waved him away with a soft smile, but said nothing and sank back into the luxurious feather bed. She'd been too tired the night before to Pay attention, but she noticed its comfort now. She fell back into the pillows, savoring her afterglow.

Their breakfast consisted of fresh squeezed orange juice accompanied by Portuguese sweetbreads fresh from the bakery next door, she was told. Seth moaned when he bit off a chunk of pure heaven, which seemed to sweeten his mood further. Seth received a text and grunted when he read it but didn't comment. They paid their bill and left the charming—full of many delights—hotel.

Outside, the wrap-around porch had been swept free from any trace of snow. Sloane spotted a round jelly-belly caretaker who had just finished shoveling the walkway and was throwing salt down. Both his nose and cheeks were as red as Rudolph's, and he wished them a sound *Merry Christmas* and winked at them as he bid them on their merry way.

Sloane felt good, refreshed, and ready to face the day despite the grim chores facing them. She figured Seth felt better, too, when she noticed a bit more pep in his step.

As they walked to the parking lot, Sloane said, "That guy would make a perfect Santa with that white beard and hair. I hope the kids see him around. I don't know how much longer Joel will believe, but he did ask if Santa would be able to find him here on Cape Cod since he's not home. He also wondered whether Monalisa had a fireplace."

Seth chuckled. "Yes, she does. Janie warns me every year not to light a fire on Christmas Eve. So I guess we still have two believers."

Once they were in the car driving back, Seth said, "Do you mind stopping at Sea Waters Medical Equipment and Supply so I can schedule delivery? Ms. de Groupe texted that she sent in the order. Doing things face-to-face may speed things up."

A bell overhead rang when Sloane opened the door to the supply store. Seth followed her in and closed the door behind him.

Saul Grossman looked up as they approached the counter. "Ah, Seth. I'm working on gathering everything you need. If you can get a space ready for set up, I can make this happen quickly." He winked. "Just need a little holiday magic."

"I need a whole lot of that." Seth rubbed the back of his neck, seeming uncomfortable. "What kind of space are we talking about?"

"Something on the ground level will be helpful, with as little furniture as possible." Saul glanced at the computer screen. "We need space for the hospital bed—"

"I thought it would help her recover if she was in her own bed."

"The caregivers and nurse need a bed that can easily be

manipulated for her care. The monitors, ventilator, and IV stand require space to accommodate the tubing, wires, etc. The hospital bed can be raised and lowered as necessary. It makes caring for the person much easier and helps with circulation and any drainage concerns. Existing bedroom furniture isn't designed for that. I'm adding compression stockings because those will help her, too."

"Yeah, you're right. I wasn't thinking . . ."

"That's why you have me. Let me see . . . Doesn't Monalisa have a parlor? Most of those old homes do. Remove the sofa and chairs. The good news is the in-home units are smaller than those in a hospital."

"How soon can you get her set up?"

"I was just checking our inventory, and I'd say several days. I'll be in touch with Fair Haven, so she'll certainly be all set well before the weekend." Saul checked the papers he held. "You've got time to prepare. I'll do everything I can to expedite things."

Seth clapped Saul on the back and shook his hand. "Thanks, man."

"You taking Janie to see Santa arrive Wednesday afternoon down at the Chatham Fish Pier?

"I forgot all about that!" He glanced at Sloane and shrugged. "I don't know . . ."

Sloane grabbed his hand. "It's still Christmas, Seth. Keep it as normal as you can. Kids need that."

"Will do."

When they left the store, Sloane said, "I've been in touch with Addie, and as a therapist, she told me the same thing. Let the kids keep Christmas. I know they've written their letters to Santa. Joel told me he went one better and sent his to God too."

Seth grinned and nodded. "Okay. Monalisa will know when Provincetown tree lighting, Chatham Christmas Sea

Stroll, and other events take place, too. I think it'll be a great diversion. We'll just tell Janie that her mom will be coming home for Christmas and leave it at that."

"Good idea. We'll play it by ear, but at least we have a plan."

"The family needs a little Christmas cheer for sure."

"We haven't decorated the tree yet, so let's line up the personnel we need for Mal and then get this Christmas started."

Chapter Four: A Tree by Any Other Name

Monday Night Before Christmas

After an exuberant greeting from Whaley, who sported reindeer antlers and a red bow attached to his collar — which he actively tried to chew off — Sloane gave Seth some time to gather himself. Their recent phone calls while she was in Michigan prepared her for his depression. Between caring for his young niece, Janie, worry over Mallory's care, Monalisa's recovery, and his healing leg, he seemed to be barely treading water.

When she'd run into him last summer after a decade's separation, he'd been so full of life and had pulled her out of her depression over losing Whitt and her fear for Joel. Their unexpected love had given her a new lease on life. But ever since Monalisa's accidental fall into the ocean and the shark attack on his leg, his positive attitude and confident ego had been replaced with despair. The news about Mallory the day before just brought another whole kettle of fish down on him.

It bothered her that he seemed to see himself not as the lifesaver he was but as less than a whole man. *What horse crap! He's anything but.* If only she could get him away and off somewhere to remind him he was more than enough man for her. However, with a recovering aunt, a seriously ill sister coming home to possibly die, and two children in the house, it'd take a proverbial Christmas miracle to raise his spirit, let alone get him back into her arms and bed. Mallory's poor prognosis made lovemaking impossible for the foreseeable future. At least Sloane had the opportunity to hold him in her arms the night before and gave him what comfort she could that morning.

She sighed, hugged her son, and watched him gallop off with Whaley and Janie.

Monalisa finished her in-home physical therapy exercises, breathing heavily as she sat in her captain's chair, which made sitting and standing easier on her recovering body. "I got your text, Sloane. I'm creating a list of Christmas events for your first Cape Cod Christmas, as you requested. I'm glad you're here. It's a beautiful season, and we Cape Codders go all out. There's plenty to keep the spirits up. Not only do we have all the decorating and baking to do, but the island also has several charming events. Wednesday afternoon, Santa arrives on the Chatham Fish Pier and the Chatham Christmas Sea Stroll begins, followed by the annual traditional tree lighting. Oh, and we have got to see Provincetown's trees."

Sloane shook her head and smiled. "Won't that be too much for one night? You see one tree, you've seen them all."

"You might just as well say *Bah Humbug*, girl. That's simply not true at all, no matter where in the world you are, but especially here on the Cape, just wait and see. All trees are magical, but there's something, uh, compelling about P-town's tree. It's another *must see* event."

Sloane coughed and straightened. "Guess I lost my Christmas spirit temporarily."

Monalisa nodded. "Understandable, but I have a fix for that. Give me a minute to round up the children." She pushed herself from the chair and called out to the kids.

Whaley arrived first, followed by the two clearly cooped-up energized children.

"Wassup?" Janie's eyes widened, and she put her hands over her giggling mouth as if amazed at what she'd said.

Monalisa quirked a brow but ignored Janie's brief foray into tweenhood. "Get your jackets. We're going on a mystery trip."

"Are we goin' whale watching?" Joel asked.

"Maybe."

Janie perked up. "Are we going to see Mom? I want to introduce Joel. She'll like him. Maybe he can wake her up."

Monalisa glanced at Joe and Sloane's strained faces. Not to betray their fears, she smiled and said, "Not now, sweety. Guess again."

Janie pouted. "Aww. It better not be grocery shopping."

"What if we're shopping for Christmas baking?" Sloane suggested.

"All right, I'm game! Where are we going?"

"You'll see soon enough. Get crackin'." Monalisa groaned. "Getting you ready and out the door is like herding cats."

Janie pulled her coat on. "I'm ready."

Whaley jumped up, wagging his tail hard enough to sweep the mail off the small entryway table.

"Down boy. Settle." Monalisa retrieved a chew and made him beg for it to distract the whale of a dog. "Works like a charm." She winked at Sloane. "Remember that. The time may come when you'll need that info." She gestured to the distressed wood floating shelf above the table and whispered, "I keep his chews in that pewter pitcher."

"Joe, get your rear end in gear. You're coming with us." Monalisa looked at Sloane. "Hop to it, Sloane. Time to go find that spirit you lost." She led them to the SUV, tossing the keys to Joe. "You're driving."

"Apparently." He smiled. "Where to?"

"Head due north."

"Route Six A or just Six?"

"Six."

"What are we looking for?"

"It's a Christmas surprise."

"Alrighty then. Christmas surprise it is," Joe said.

Monalisa smiled at seeing his mood seemingly lifting a bit.

Sloane felt her spirits rise, too. After all, Christmas was the perfect time for surprises, dreams, wishes, and most of all hope. Maybe there was a chance everything would be okay.

She was thrilled at recognizing where they were as Seth drove into Provincetown. They approached McMillian Pier, and Seth pulled into the familiar pricy parking lot across from the bus terminal.

Joel got excited when he recognized where they were. "This is where all the rad things are!"

"What's so cool about it?" Janie questioned, since having grown up on Cape Cod she'd probably seen almost every attraction.

"There are these things where you stick your head in and can be in a pirate picture or Jaw's mouth and The Pirate Museum!" He paused. "I never got to go there because of, you know, the shark and everything . . ."

A brief shadow passed over everyone at the memory of the shark attack that plagued both Seth and Monalisa.

Monalisa nudged Joel and in her best Godfather accent, she said, "Fuhgeddaboudit. We'll go one day, but it's Christmas, so keep walking. There's something way cooler to see."

Mixed in with the sea salt air was the delicious scent of — roasting hotdogs! Sloane's stomach growled.

"Looks like John is hosting a hot dog roast again this year. We can grab a few footlongs," Seth said.

Dusk shaded the sky as they approached Lopes Square,

21

where Sloane faced the wackiest Christmas tree she had ever seen!

"Look, Mom, a lobster pot tree! It looks like a pyramid. Sick!"

Sloane was surprised at the sight but delighted to see Joel so excited.

The structure was made entirely of lobster traps. Fishnets laced with lights helped keep the squat pyramid of the tree together. Huge fake lobsters and large red bows served as ornaments, and the tree topper consisted of two brightly lit lobster traps with a sparkling arrangement of bright buoys reaching for the sky. The icy temperature formed glittering icicles on the pots, adding to its haunting beauty when the lights came on.

However, it was the image of her sea savior smiling that held her attention. Seth looked better than he had earlier.

Seth turned to her, planting a soft kiss on her lips and drawing her into his warmth. The look in his eyes melted her, making the blood racing through her veins throb with desire. He made her feel all Christmasy and happy.

Seth's breath tickled her ears as he whispered, "When I was in the Service, I saw the El Castillo pyramid in Chichen Itza and always figured if they lit it up for Christmas, it would look like our lobster pot tree."

Sloane smiled. "I haven't been there, but this is great. That nautical tree topper is fabulous."

"It's made with buoys. Pretty clever, eh? Artist Julian Popko first created the tree in two-thousand-four, and the local lobstermen have donated traps and trappings for the past decade or so. It's become a community venture."

The kids pulled their phones out and snapped many selfies of their looniest looks and poses with the tree as a background.

Then Joel placed his hand on his belly and announced, "I'm

starved, Mom, can we eat?"

"Hot dog, anyone?" Monalisa had apparently slipped off and returned carrying a box piled with hot dogs. She led them to a long picnic bench across from John's Foot Long, and everyone grabbed a hot dog.

Seth waved his hot dog at the building. "In the summer, we eat at John's Foot Long restaurant on the upper deck. The view is great."

Monalisa, between bites, said, "Wonder what the first Pilgrims who landed here would think about these dogs?"

Sloane sat up straight and laughed. "Good question. I'd forgotten the Pilgrims landed here."

Monalisa nodded. "They sure did. A lot of history here in Provincetown."

Joel nudged Janie. "In good ole P-town. Bet all that water out there" — he pointed toward the sea — "made them want to pee."

"Eew, gross," Janie groused. "Lame joke."

"And poop, too." Joel giggled. "It's a pee and poop P-town!"

Seth jumped in with, "Good thing we're not in Fartmouth."

"Ha, ha. Pewy but funny," Janie said. "It's Falmouth, Uncle Joe."

Sloane smothered a motherly grin that she didn't want Joel to see. She debated discussing his bathroom humor and then decided to let it go. *Boys, men, and bathroom issues. Sheesh.*

They'd sat awhile enjoying the festive ambiance when a group of men all clad in red Speedos and Santa hats raced toward the Pier, yelling loudly as they jumped into the Atlantic Ocean. Their screeches could be heard after they hit the cold water.

"What on earth!" Sloane gaped at Seth and Monalisa, trying to figure out what just happened.

Monalisa chuckled. "I told you this would be a Christmas surprise. That was the Speedo Christmas Run and Polar Plunge, so you're getting several P-town celebrations simultaneously. The run and plunge is part of what makes P-town, P-town. Be sure to go to Pilgrim's Monument and you'll see another festive feature. Try saying that three times."

Sloane stood and looked. Indeed, the monument was decorated as yet another P-town tree of sorts. Long strands of Christmas lights skirted the towering structure, creating another tree of lights. What a delight.

Carolers stopped near where they sat in Lopes Square singing Jingle Bells with gusto. The kids and adults joined the Christmas chorus. Even Seth. All in all, Monalisa's outing achieved its goal, they were all happily distracted with Christmas cheer. They drove home singing and laughing, calling it a night after reaching the house.

CHAPTER FIVE: DOWN ON THE FARM

Tuesday Before Christmas

Sloane was enjoying her morning coffee when Seth joined her.

He poured a cup of coffee and sat next to her at the table. "Looks like the ragamuffins are sleeping in."

She nodded. "All that bracing sea air and all the events tired them out. Don't worry. All too soon, they'll be rushing in here, raring to go. By the way, don't you put up a Christmas tree?" She cast her gaze around the room. Save for the wreath on the door and lights rimming the mantle that held a nautical Nativity set, the house was practically devoid of Christmas.

"Monalisa wanted to wait for you to get here. Trying to hold Janie off wasn't easy, so we just put out a few things."

She chuckled. "I know what you mean. Joel has been champing at the bit for Christmas to get here."

"But to answer your question, we go all out under normal circumstances. A tree, lights, inflatables . . ."

Sloane laughed. "Don't tell me you put out the alligator and flamingo water toys from *Seaberry Souvenir Shack*? And add a big red bow around the necks?"

Seth laughed and shrugged. "Not quite."

Overjoyed to see Seth's mood improve, Sloane kept the banter going. "Do you use our banana boat for the sleigh?"

Seth ignored her remarks and continued. "I found the perfect outdoor blow-ups. Wait until Joel sees them." He snapped his fingers. "I've got an idea. How about we go to the tree farm and cut down our tree."

"Great! Joel has never done that, and quite frankly, neither have I. That'll be fun. Whitt wasn't into natural trees because of his allergies. He worried about the ecology, too."

Seth paused, staring at her. *Just his gaze, mixed with rocking those laugh lines, gets me hot every time.*

A beat later, he said, "Tree farms are sustainable." He winked. "They're good oxygen and negative ions producers while capturing carbon dioxide, so no worries."

She leaned over to kiss him. "I love it when you go all environmental on me."

"There's a lot more I can do *on* you, lady," he whispered against her lips.

Sloane smiled, glancing at the telltale bulge of his shaft. "Do tell." A host of hot fantasies flitter through her mind.

They were busy canoodling when the children exploded into the room.

"Eww, yuck." Joel wasn't much into public displays of affection.

Janie was another story. "Miss Sloane and Uncle Joe sitting in a tree, k-i-s-s-i-n-g . . ."

Sloane and Seth separated and giggled.

"What are we doing today?" Joel asked, bouncing on his toes.

"I thought we'd go to Cs," Seth announced.

Joel's face fell. "Sounds boooring."

Janie whooped and clapped her hands. "C's Christmas Tree Farm is not boring."

Joel frowned. "What's a Christmas tree farm?"

Janie cocked her head. "Seriously?"

"Uh, yeah. Never heard of a farm for trees."

"Tree farms grow Christmas trees like farmers grow crops, silly," Janie explained. "We call it farming trees. You go through a forest of trees, find the perfect one, cut it down, and bring it home. Like in the old-fashioned days."

Joel made chopping motions and said, "You mean chop it down with a humongous ax like Paul Bunyon? Whaley can be our Blue Ox."

Whaley lifted his head and woofed his agreement.

Seth laughed. "We use a saw, actually."

Sloane added. "Joel's been studying Tall Tales in school, as you just heard. Paul Bunyan is a tale that sprang from up north. Minnesota, I believe."

Janie pouted, "Why don't we talk about Paul Bunyon in school? We got gypped."

"Arrgh," Joel responded in his best pirate accent. "Cuz, matey, you be studying pirates like Black Sam Bellamy and Blackbeard."

"Oh yeah." Janie giggled.

Sloane set out cereal, milk, and bowls. "How about you kids eat your breakfast and get ready for a Christmas tree hunt?"

"Let's race," Joel suggested. "I bet I finish mine before you do."

The children raced through breakfast and were ready to go in record time.

The trip to C's took a while, but Seth didn't mind driving. The children were happily discussing what the perfect tree should look like while he and Sloane hammered their way through the merits of a balsam versus a scotch pine tree. They both ruled out a Douglas Fir since it wasn't indigenous to the island. When Seth noted Pitch Pine was grown naturally there, he almost laughed at Sloane's expression.

She protested. "Pitch Pine is bent and scraggly."

"I agree." He turned onto the road with a sign saying *Coonamessett Bog Tree Farm*.

Sloane looked at the sign and laughed. "I can see why you call it C's. That's a mouthful."

Seth parked the van while Sloane gathered the kids. They were met by a teen dressed in boots, a buffalo plaid wool jacket, and heavy gloves. He carried a saw and an ax, much to Joel's delight. He explained how the tree farm was laid out and outlined the safety precautions.

It was getting colder, and the kids began fussing, anxious to start looking for their tree. The young man distracted them with promises to let them help cut down their choice. Seth continued the debate with Sloane on the pros of scotch pine versus balsa.

Sloane turned to the teen and appealed to his experience. "What do you think?"

Seth chimed in before the teen could reply. "This is the best tree farm around. They cultivate the best of the bunch and protect them from the winds. You'll be happy with whatever we pick, I promise."

The teen shrugged and nodded. "What he said."

"Okay then. Scotch pine it is."

Seth blew out a breath once the decision was made because it prevented an inspection of both tree sections. He didn't think any of them could handle a long hunt in the frigid temperatures.

The teen led them to the area, and the search for the perfect tree began. Seth and Sloane decided to let the kids choose, only offering their opinion as to good or bad. After looking at what seemed like a million trees, he noticed the tree farm worker chuckling at the banter among the group.

"This is a good one."

"How about this one?"

"That tree is bare in the back."

"Your tree looks like a lobster pot, low and squat.

"That tree is too tall."

"Looks like a Charlie Brown Christmas tree."

"Your tree is too small."

"In a word. No."

The winds picked up, the sky clouded, and snowflakes began to cover the trees. Just when Seth thought they'd all freeze like popsicles, a break in the clouds opened, and a sunbeam bathed a lone Scotch Pine, revealing a shimmering piece of natural perfection. He saw everyone gaping at the sight.

"This one's just right." They said in unison, then laughed.

Seth agreed it was indeed *thee* perfect tree for them. He and the farm worker cleared the bottom branches, and true to the young man's promise, Janie and Joel got to help use the saw, and Joel was allowed to add the final chop with the ax to topple the tree. Everyone grabbed hold to drag the tree back through the woods to the tree prep area.

Seth got a kick out of watching Joel squeal in delight as the tree was put in what he called a tree shaker and then through a tunnel that tightly bound it with plastic netting. While he handled the payment and tied the tree to the car rack, Sloane led the kids to the stand serving hot chocolate. By time he joined them, Joel's cup was filled with big, fluffy marshmallows, and as usual, Janie chose mini-green marshmallows in hopes it'd make the Grinch happy.

Janie frowned at Joel. "You have more marshmallows than cocoa."

"Do not."

"Do too."

Sloane ended the discussion by pointing out the goats in a nearby pen. That did the trick.

Seth settled for a to-go cup of cocoa and let the kids play with the goats for a bit before they left for home.

On the drive to the house, he called his friends, Hank and Jake, asking them to stop by and help deal with the tree. His leg was acting up, and he wasn't sure he could do it himself. *Thank God for Hank and Jake.*

While clearing the space for the tree, Seth was struck with a sudden thought. After the shark attack, he had learned that Hank had taken physical therapy courses during the off-season and became a certified technician. He'd helped both Seth and Monalisa during their recoveries. *Thank God he's here, I need to talk to him about helping Mal.*

CHAPTER SIX: HOME FOR THE HOLIDAY

Wednesday Morning Before Christmas

The next morning, Seth escorted Janie and Joel out to Jake's van, filled with a few other kids. They were off on a Christmas Candy Cane Adventure sponsored by the ever-popular local candy shop.

"Thanks for taking them in, Jake," he said. "We'll pick them up this afternoon."

"No problem, Seth. As you can see, I have a few other ta-galongs. I'll see ya later."

While the children were away, Sloane and Monalisa helped him rearranged the furniture in the parlor to prepare for the hospital bed and Mallory's homecoming. Fortunately, the powder room was nearby, making things easier and conven-ient. Monalisa set the round table with a hurricane lamp off to the side to use as a nightstand while Seth and Sloane moved the settee and matching needlepoint chairs to the wide and long hallway. They could always be added back to the room if there was room. Monalisa removed the knickknacks from the mantel so the space could be used for medications and an-ything else they might need. Once they were done, there was plenty of room for the hospital bed to be accessible on all sides. Seth pushed a chest of drawers against the far wall but left enough room for the ventilator and other equipment.

They were in the kitchen eating lunch when Seth's phone pinged with a text. Delivery had moved up to that afternoon due to the holiday season. He figured Saul had managed to

31

move things along faster than expected. *Now, to figure out what to tell Janie. How do I prepare her?* Seth broached the subject with Monalisa.

"Janie's a smart cookie. She'll know the score when she sees the equipment arrive. When there's more to tell, we'll tell her. Right now, we bring Mal home and — "

"I know, I know. Hope for the best."

Monalisa picked up the empty lunch dishes and placed them in the dishwasher. "Coffee or tea?"

"Coffee," he and Sloane said at the same time.

Seth's phone buzzed with another text. The equipment was en route. While he waited, he and Sloane assembled the inflatables and set up the display in the front yard. Everything was ready, and he couldn't wait for the kids to see the display when they got home. He chuckled because he'd added one that Janie knew nothing about. *She needs all the happiness I can provide.*

"Perfect. Now, all we need is Mallory." Hope rose unbidden, and he felt amazingly optimistic. *There's no place like home to heal.*

CHAPTER SEVEN: THERE COMES SANTA CLAUSE

Wednesday Afternoon & Evening Before Christmas

Sloane had just settled on the sofa to cuddle with Seth when his cell chirped again.

He looked at the text and then at her. "Do you mind picking the kids up from the candy shop and then taking them down to the Chatman Fish Pier? Santa's arrival is at one o'clock. This text says the equipment will be delivered soon. With the traffic, I don't think I can make it there and back in time."

Sloane couldn't help but tease. "So . . . does Santa arrive in a helicopter and land on the sea? That'd be unique, for sure. I've never seen that."

He threw her a disparaging look. "I wanted to go with you guys, but —"

She hushed him with a quick kiss. "I know the way. I better get started. Hmm, I can see it all now. A winter *water*-land complete with Santa and his sleigh with whales or dolphins instead of reindeer."

Seth chuckled. "That's not how Santa comes to the islands."

"What? Does he water ski in?"

"You'll see."

She threw on her jacket and retrieved the fob from the shelf holding Whaley's chews. Traffic was a bear, but the candy

33

shop was on Main Street. There was no hope of avoiding paying through the nose for parking, but it was a small price to pay for the memories they'd make.

It didn't take her long to find the shop. She just had to follow the parents and grandparents retrieving their highly sugared children. She didn't mind because seeing her son so animated once again made her smile from ear to ear.

Joel was hopping like a kangaroo when she found them. "That was dope, Mom! I made my very own candy cane, see?" He showed her a somewhat off candy cane. The stripes were not quite right.

Janie piped up, "You cheated. You made yours crooked on purpose."

Sloane quirked her brow. "Huh?"

Janie hurried to explain. "You get to eat the ones that don't come out right. Someone's gonna have a big ole bellyache for Christmas."

"Or a million cavities." Sloane moaned. "I see a trip to the dentist in Joel's future."

"It was worth it. Besides, it's not that easy." Joel launched into an explanation of how to make a candy cane. "They even gave us the recipe so we can make our own at home."

"Wonderful." Sloane ushered them out the door and followed the crowd to the dock where Santa was due to land.

And land he did, but not by helicopter. Instead, he arrived by Coast Guard cutter. A dingy bearing a Christmas tree and his ever-present elves followed in its wake.

"Ho, ho, ho! Avast ye mateys, Merry Christmas." Santa disembarked and distributed — what else — candy canes before departing for his cottage aboard a fire engine, with sirens blaring. Before he left, he bellowed, "I'll see you tonight for the start of the annual Christmas by the Sea Stroll. It will run until Christmas Eve." Then he launched into another round of ho-ho-ho-ing. "I'll be busy preparing for Christmas Eve, but some of my elves will be on hand. Have you ever heard my elves sing?" Santa wagged a warning finger. "Don't forget. I'll see you all at Santa's parade, and then we light the tree in Sears Park. See you there." As the fire engine began to move away, Santa looked at Joel and winked, then gave him a thumbs up.

Joel's eyes nearly popped out of his head, rounded in amazement. His mouth opened and closed before he said. "Janie, did you see that? He winked at us! Gave us a thumbs up, too."

Janie nodded. "It's a sign."

"We'll get our wish. I'm positive. Why else would he wink directly at us? "

A huge smile curled Janie's lip.

Sloane corralled the kids, separating them from the bustling crowd. "I think we should head home now so we can come back for the sea stroll and tree lightning later tonight."

They retrieved their car and headed home. Sloane chuckled when she parked the car and noticed both kids had fallen asleep. She woke them, hoping Monalisa had supper waiting.

Seth planted a heart-stopping welcome home kiss on her lips and pulled her aside. "They just finished setting up the equipment. If you don't mind going to the Christmas Stroll and tree lighting with the kids, I can let Fair Haven know we're all set for Mal's transfer home."

After dinner, just Sloane and the children headed to Main Street for the Santa Parade, Christmas by the Sea Stroll, and tree lighting in Sears Park. A friend reserved a spot for them outside his charming two-story restaurant at the end of the street close to the park. His eatery was lit from port to stern with white lights, giving them front-row views of the amazingly festive sight.

Wreaths hung from old turn-of-the-century streetlamps,

lights twisted around tree trunks lining the street. No shop, church, monument, or steeple was left undecorated or unlit. Santa tossed handfuls of well-formed candy canes, no doubt donated by the local candy shop to the crowds of happy on-lookers.

Carolers, bands, and a super tall angel — literally on stilts — led Santa and his fire engine straight down Main Street. A host of elves flanked the fire truck, revving up the crowds and urging merriment with their elfish tricks, adding a festive flare.

When the parade reached the entrance to Sears Park, Santa lifted a bullhorn to bellow, "Ho, ho, ho, and Merry Christmas to one and all. I'll be grabbing a cup of hot cocoa while you begin the Chatham Christmas Sea Stroll. Remember, each shop has something special in store for your children. Parents and grandparents, you can shop while the children collect their treasures. Children will get a piece of a puzzle for each shop you visit. Wait and see what you win when you put all the pieces together and cash in at *Pieces Puzzles Shoppe*. I'll meet you all back at Sears Park for the annual tree lighting. Children, be sure to fill those Santa Sacks my helpful elves are passing out."

Joel and Janie took their sacks remembering to say *Thank you* and *Merry Christmas*, and off they went. Sloane followed along, trying to keep up.

Besides the puzzle pieces, the kids collected quite a treasure trove of goodies. Whale Tales gave them a bookmark, Sands Bank and Loan distributed sand dollar ornaments, Cape Cod Sock Shop gave out Christmas stockings, Snip N Shore Hair Care gave Santa headbands, antlers, or angel halos, and *Cake Cod Bake N Take* offered cake pop samples with mini-Santa caps, which Janie thought was adorable, to name a few.

Children, parents, and grandparents joined the strolling

carolers, singing every version known to mankind of Jingle Bells. Bustling elves flittered through the crowds, encouraging everyone to sing along.

Finally, the circuit was finished, and after a rousing rendition of Santa Claus is Coming to Town, the countdown for the tree lighting began. When the crowd shouted *three*, the lights on the huge town Christmas tree topped by a huge starfish came on, and so did all the lights on the sculptures throughout the park. A hush fell over the crowd as if by magic while the band played Oh Christmas Tree. Sloane could practically feel the goodwill flowing through the air.

The delightful elves began juggling illuminated globes. The salty sea breeze carried the delectable aromas of chocolate and cinnamon, urging everyone toward the firepit where roasting chestnuts, marshmallows, hot cocoa, and cider, as well as s'mores tickled their taste buds, noses, and tummies.

Despite all that, the crisp clean scent of evergreen reached Sloane, and strong arms suddenly encircled her. She looked over her shoulder to see Seth in a Santa hat.

Seth kissed her tenderly before saying, "I couldn't let you see your first Cape Cod Christmas Tree ceremony without being with you. Merry Christmas, Sloane, I love you."

I love the heat of his palm, especially since I'm freezing my buns off. Okay, I love the feel of his hands on me anytime. She buried herself in his embrace, which was abruptly interrupted. The children had put their puzzle pieces together and found they had each won a free s'more. After copious amounts of sugary goodness, everyone was ready to head home.

Seth carried a sleepy Joel, whose tired head lolled against Seth's heart. Sloane held onto Janie's hand as they walked to the parking lot. It was the end of a very special night, but surprises awaited the kid at the house. Snowflakes fell softly as they walked back to their respective vehicles, and Seth led the way home.

CHAPTER EIGHT: SURPRISE

Wednesday Night Before Christmas

As Seth got closer to the house, he pushed the remote, and the inflatable Santa Pirate—complete with his ship, eyepatch, and Jolly Roger flag—sprang up on the lawn. Sloane and Joel pulled into the driveway behind them. He almost laughed at the shocked expressions on the kids' faces.

He spread his arms and intoned, "Arrgh, ho-ho-ho ye mateys!"

Janie and Joel yelled *Awesome!*, jumping around with excitement. Monalisa released Whaley, who joined the kids, barking up a storm as they checked all the displays.

They finally entered the house, pulling off hats, reindeer antlers, headbands, mittens, and jackets as they went inside. Seth had made a fire in the fireplace before he left the house, so the house was toasty warm. With little fanfare, he pressed a finger to his lips and led everyone to the parlor door. He mentally crossed his fingers and held his breath, hoping he was doing this right. *Too late now. Hafta wing it.* He almost laughed at his pun. For a pilot with a business called *Wing It*, he had to admit it was pretty decent.

The room was all set, and Mallory was home. Surprisingly, everything fit perfectly, and the equipment didn't make the awful noises they made in the rehab center. Seth wondered why but was very grateful. Again, he thanked heaven for the caregivers, equipment, and the opportunity to bring his precious sister home for the holidays. His Christmas wish was that she would heal and wake up.

He silently prayed for a Christmas miracle. *Please, please, please,. Lord God. I promise I will not ask you to make me whole again. I can live just fine with pain and my limp, just heal Mal.*

When he opened the door, light spilled from a tiny bedside Christmas tree, and Mallory lay silently in the bed. But there were no words, no prior experiences or moments that prepared him—or anyone else—for Janie's response when she came through the door.

She froze in the doorway and stared, then a look of pure unadulterated joy burst across her face. "Mama! Mama, you're home." She ran to her mom's bedside with a deluge of what he hoped were happy tears flowing down her cheeks. She looked at her mom with the widest, happiest smile he'd ever seen on her. She looked like she did on Christmas morning, but better.

Amid Whaley's excited barking and Janie's happy sobs, it was all Seth could manage not to break down himself, fighting back the tears making his eyes sting. He would never forget the look of joy on Janie's face. Sloane moved to his side and slipped her arm through his, her own eyes filling with tears. Monalisa cried openly but softly, looking like she was praying through her tears and fears.

"Merry Christmas, everyone," he called out.

Seth didn't rush the homecoming, didn't prevent the hub-bub, didn't quiet Whaley. On the contrary, he let the excitement fill the room and saturate their souls, let it spread the magic of Mal's homecoming, and most importantly, he allowed it to linger. His family needed this positive energy, this happiness. Instead of insisting everyone be calm, fearing it was too much or overly stimulating and harmful for Mallory, he treasured the moment, letting the warmth of all of the positive vibes flow freely.

For him, the moment became a pocket of promise and hope, joy and warmth, love and communion permitting, even encouraging, a sense of relief, a respite from his ever-present anguish that accompanied Mal's condition. He deliberately quashed any brotherly cautions to quiet everyone or to prohibit touching Mallory. He didn't stop the kisses, didn't bring up bedtime, no, he let it all play out. He felt the love from every single person in the room flow freely, enveloping and embracing Mal, and hoped its healing powers penetrated the fog that had been holding her a prisoner. Through all his pathos, pain, and agony, he felt bolstered by Sloane's presence, her support, her empathy. He ignored the tears coursing down his face, bowed his head, and prayed, *Thank you, Father.*

Slowly, one by one, at their own pace, each family member left the room. However, Whaley remained, planting himself beside Mallory's bed. For once, no one called him away from his post. Indeed, he set the stage for everyone else, an unspoken pledge not to leave Mal alone. Seth left the parlor room door open, making that room a part of whatever the days ahead might bring. He vowed the parlor would be a portal of connection. Mal had had enough isolation.

Thursday Before Christmas

In the morning, Seth found Janie asleep at the foot of her mother's bed. Whaley followed him out of the parlor and whined to go outside. Seth rubbed the faithful dog's head, praising him, "You're a good boy. Who's a good watchdog? You are." He let Whaley outside and turned to head for the kitchen.

Janie stirred and roused. She planted a kiss on Mallory's forehead before she bounced out of the room filled with apparent energy. "Where's my iPad?"

"Precisely wherever you left it." Monalisa joined them wearing her smock. "There's fresh coffee, Joe. Ready for some? There's oatmeal, too."

Janie snapped her fingers. "Oh yeah. I remember where it is! I left it in the living room." She scampered off to retrieve it.

Joel must have heard her — she was not known for a quiet start to the day. She was the proverbial morning person, while Joel was the opposite.

Joel emerged from his room rubbing his eyes and dragged his flannel PJ-clad body to the couch next to Janie. He looked at her screen. "What are you searching for?"

"Oh, co . . . co-ma," he said, sounding out the word. "What's that?"

"It's what my mom is in. A *coma-toes* state."

Joel giggled. "I thought she was in Massachusetts."

"It means sleeping, dingbat."

"You already know that. What are you searching Dr. Google for? Be careful. Dr. Google might give you cooties." He lunged at her and wiggled his fingers. "I'll help you scratch your cooties."

Janie yelped.

Seth shook his head at their antics as he answered the knock on the front door and then led the health aide lady to the parlor. He stood in the doorway, facing the living room while the woman bathed Mallory.

Janie grumbled. "There's got to be stuff we can do to get her to wake up."

Joel scratched his head. "You mean like smelling salts."

"I think they tried that already.'

"Try holding pepper under her nose then."

"She'll sneeze."

"That will wake her up." Joel looked certain it was a great plan.

"You might be on to something! It says here to *stimulate* her five senses." She snapped her fingers. "I know. Let's list them and figure out what will wake her up."

"Hm, touch is a sense. Let's tickle her toes. That always

41

works for me. That's what Mom does to wake me up."

"Good idea!" They slipped from the couch and padded toward the parlor.

Seth held up his hand. "Hold on, kids." He glanced over his shoulder to see the health aide smoothing the sheets over Mallory. The washcloth lay crumpled on the bedside table. "Okay, you can go in now."

"Hi guys, I'm Amy Bolton," the health aide said. "You two here to help take care of Sleeping Beauty?"

The kids looked at each other, then Janie said, "We are. We're going to try tickling her toes."

"Be my guest."

"You mean it?"

"For sure. That's part of my job, and you can help. We call it Sensory Stimulation." She took a small wheeled tool and ran it over Mallory's body.

Joel gaped and spoke to Janie out of the side of his mouth. "That oughta wake her up. That's a wicked-looking thing."

Mallory didn't move.

Janie started chattering away in a sing-song voice. "Hi, Mom, welcome home. We're going to wake you up. Wake up, sleepyhead, wake up. Santa came to Cape Cod by boat. It was way rad."

Joel put his hands over his ears. "That would wake Rip Van Winkle."

"Who's he?"

"He's a dude who slept for twenty years. Didn't you learn about him in school?"

"Guess not." Janie lifted the sheet at Mallory's feet.

Joel cried out and began wiggling his fingers on Mallory's toes. "Tickle, tickle, tickle, make your toes wiggle."

A toe moved.

Joel's eyes rounded. "Did you see that? She moved!" He turned and yelled, "Mr. Joe, Miss Mallory moved her toe.

We're gonna wake her up.

Janie tried tickling. "Do it again, Mom. I'll tickle you awake."

But nothing more happened.

Janie was undeterred. "Okay, we'll try another sense. Hearing. Let's make a Christmas playlist of her favorite carols."

They scampered off to do just that.

Monalisa came in to check on all the ruckus.

Amy shook her head and said, "Those kids are something else, but do anything you can. Talking, singing, music, and smells can keep her senses operating."

Monalisa smiled. "Then we are going to flood this house with a bevy of heavenly smells."

Amy smiled. "I see you have a tree set up. That fresh pine will help."

"The kids want to decorate the whole house," Seth said. "Maybe we should start with Mallory's room."

"It won't hurt, and it'll give the children a way to help."

Half an hour later, the children came in with Malory's Christmas music playlist.

Janie announced, "Her favorite is Jingle Bell Rock. I found lots of versions of it. Maybe that will wake her up. At Fair Haven, there was no *'imulation.'*"

Amy laughed. "What you mean is stimulation. It can't hurt." As she prepared to leave, she said, "The home nurse will be Ursula Andrews. She's jolly and a hoot. She brings good energy."

As the morning wore on, Seth couldn't believe the host of caregivers who descended upon the household. The last to arrive was Hank.

"I'm here on two counts," Hank announced. "The primary is as Mal's physical therapist, working her muscles twice a day. I'll also be using some holistic methods with lotions and minerals, including frankincense."

Joe perked up. "Like what the Three Wise Men brought! Do you have gold, too?"

Hank chuckled. "Sorry, gold is not part of her treatment."

Joel looked crestfallen but brightened when Hank added, "I've got exercises for her that are worth her weight in gold, though. By the way, they call frankincense *King's oil* because the Three Kings brought it with them. It's said it can fix what ails ya."

Janie looked up from her iPad, and all the phones in the room chimed as if on cue. "I've made a schedule for all of us to keep Mom company. You can talk to her, sing to her, tell jokes, and bring her things to smell. Aunt Monalisa and I are adding different essential oils for her diffuser."

Hank nodded. "Essential scents like eucalyptus, peppermint, tea tree, pepper—"

"See Janie? I told you pepper could wake her up," Joel announced.

"Along with parsley. sage, rosemary, and thyme, too?" Janie chirped.

Hank laughed. "I like that folksong too! Most of those oils work. I'll be using twelve essential oils. And if you add classical music, drumming, Indian and Japanese music, that can help, too. Everything vibrates with energy, so if you can find some music frequencies around 285 Hertz, that will help."

"Huh?" Joel said.

"On it," Janie said.

Seth looked at Janie's message as she left to do more research. "According to the schedule, it's my turn to visit with Mallory."

Hank looked at him and said, "Believe it or not, Janie's on the right track. I'm using every trick in the book. Massage, music therapy, aromatherapy, anything to stimulate the brain. Don't knock it." He used hand sanitizer as he prepared to leave. "I'll be back about eight o'clock if that's okay with you?"

"Great. Thanks. I noticed that you put the tree lights up yesterday, I appreciate it."

Hank snorted. "Monalisa would skin me alive if it wasn't all set to trim. I've been doing it for years."

"How do you deal with the god-awful tricky lights?"

Hank winked. "Buy 'em new."

"Every year?"

"You betcha."

Seth chuckled and clapped Hank on the back. "Dude."

They laughed, and Seth pulled a chair next to Mallory's bed as Hank donned his jacket and left the room.

He watched Mallory breathe for a few moments before saying, "Mallory Marie Bradford Davies. You wake up now. We're moving heaven and earth to bring you outta your brain fog." He kept his tone firm so she'd know he meant business. "And Janie needs you. You'd be proud of her. She's ordering us to chat you up and stimulate the hell out of you. Soak up the love, sister, and wake up." He paused for a heartbeat. "Remember how you love fresh ground Kona coffee? I'm bringing a coffeemaker in here so you can—pardon the cliche— wake up and smell the coffee." Then he just chatted about how she'd brought some home from her Hawaiian honeymoon and got him hooked on the brew. "Thank you very much. Those beans are expensive." He left the room and returned with the coffeemaker. He set it on the mantlepiece and let it brew. He filled a pill cup with some ground coffee beans and placed it close to her nose.

Monalisa relieved Seth about an hour later. Then Janie and Joel followed for their turn. Janie started chattering, telling her mother how she was decorating the room to wake her up. She carried pine branches that she placed around the room to bring in the wonderful smells and added fiberoptic snowmen on the bedside table. "For your eyes, Mom. Gotta get all your five senses going. Hank says he's gonna be using twelve oils, too, and rubbing you down with lemon seed and orange oil. Don't worry, he'll be gentle. We got your favorite Christmas music playing, and I'm learning about classical music, so get set for a . . . um . . ."

Monalisa chuckled as she came back into the room. "I think *symphony* is the word you're looking for."

"Yeah. That's it." Janie hung a stocking from the mantle. "I got this free from the Sock Shop at the Sea Stroll, Mom. Santa will find it here on the fireplace. Plus, we're leaving the door open so you can hear everything. It's lookin' like Christmas around here. Did you know we cut our tree down? I'll tell you all about the Christmas tree farm . . ." Which she did in detail.

Joel agreed and added, "It's almost Christmas and we're just about done decorating everything."

"At least Mom's room is done."

"Skedaddle now, Janie. I got this." Monalisa winked. "Have you and Joel discussed your idea for dinner yet?"

"Partly." Janie pulled Joel out of the room and into the foyer so no one would hear them.

CHAPTER NINE: PARENT TRAP

Thursday Before Christmas

"I've got an idea," Janie whispered. "What if we plan a real romantic night for Uncle Joe and your mom? Kinda get them thinking about getting hitched and giving you a dad and family."

"I like the fam part, but I miss my real dad."

Janie patted his shoulder. "Uncle Joe can be your fake Dad."

Joel perked up. "That would work." He began to get into it. "I know! I know what we can do. I'll be a server, and you cook the dinner. We'll have music and candles."

Janie nodded. "Yup. The whole thing. Flowers 'n—"

"It's winter. Where are we gonna get flowers?"

"Ta-da!" Janie grabbed the poinsettia from the entry table. "This oughta work. Come on. Let's set the table. We can have candles, too."

Joel shook his head. "Can't play with matches."

"There's fake light candlesticks in the windows. We'll borrow them."

"Won't Monalisa be mad? We're moving all her stuff."

"Not if we clean up afterward. Come on. I'll get the fancy placemats." Janie led the way through the house to the dining room. She opened the mahogany hutch drawer, removing the holiday linens. "Wrap the silverware in the napkins," she ordered.

Joel complied.

"Not like that." Janie moved, and the silverware clattered to the floor. "Sh! Be careful."

"You bumped into me, and they fell."

"Sorry. My bad."

Joel put the silverware in the center and rolled them in the napkin like a burrito.

"That looks like a sloppy snake. Do it like this."

Joel snickered. "Looks like a hot dog. What's on the menu?"

"Oh yeah, we hafta make paper or cardboard menus for them. Good reminder."

"No, what are we cooking?"

"Umm. Hm. I can't cook."

"Me neither."

"What can you make?"

"Toast. Hm . . ." Joel paused for a minute, hand to his head. "Okay. We can work with that. On the cooking show Kid Chefs, they talked about toast points. We'll make toast, and I know how to tear up lettuce for a salad."

Janie tilted her head, thinking. "Good. I'm not allowed to use knives, though."

"We can make the toast with a side of cinnamon sugar, butter, peanut butter, and jelly . . ."

Janie snapped her fingers. "I'm allowed to use a butter knife. We can cut teeny-tiny toast triangles to make it pretty and special."

"Too bad we can't make grilled cheese sandwiches in the microwave. I'm allowed to use that."

"What will desert be?"

"Candy Canes? We know how to make them."

"Right. And I know Aunt Monalisa will be making Christmas cookies this morning . . ."

"That's fire!"

Again, she nodded. "When you do your waiter thing, it

will be perfect. I've got a tea towel for you to put on your arm like a real waiter. Don't forget, wear dark pants, a white shirt, my vest, and Uncle Joe's bow tie for the whole outfit."

"Got it."

"Remember to hum the Here Comes the Bride song when you bring the food."

"Okay, but I still wish we knew how to cook."

"Yeah. It's hard when we can't even use the stove."

"Toast triangles and PBJ will just have to do." Joel winked. "Operation Parent Wedding is a go. Shake on it." He extended his hand to seal the deal.

She shook on it. "I think we should call it Operation Parent Trap, like the movie." She giggled.

Monalisa stuck her head through the kitchen door. "Joel? Janie? Time to make Christmas cookies. They're not going to make themselves. Shake a leg."

"Coming, Aunt Monalisa," Janie said.

"Aye, aye, Cap'n," Joel cried. "Arrgh. Shiver me timbers, I'll be shakin' me pegleg."

Monalisa chuckled and tied bib aprons over the kids when they joined her at the kitchen counter. "Janie, fetch me the eggs. Then get the big mixing bowls while I get the rest of the fixins' for the sugar cookie dough."

Joel climbed on a stool to reach the countertop, and Janie bent to the cabinet beneath the counter, pulling out two mixing bowls. Then she fetched a carton of eggs from the fridge.

Monalisa smiled. "Joel, have you ever made cookies with your mother?"

Joel nodded. "Yes, Miss Monalisa."

"Excellent. I've measured out the flour, salt, and baking powder, so you just need to add them to the bowl and mix them together. Here's a whisk to use. Janie, you can mix the butter and sugar in the other bowl, and then we'll add in the eggs and vanilla. After that, we'll add the dry to the wet, and voilà, cookie dough is ready to go."

Joel said, "I mix the dry stuff, and Janie will do the wet. I got it."

Janie lifted the hand mixer after mixing all the wet ingredients. The still-rotating beater splattered the gooey mixture over Joey. He automatically retaliated by—accidentally, on purpose—dumping the flour into the mixing bowl harder than necessary. The action caused a cloud of flour dust to fly, coating each child, the counter, and the floor. It looked like a food fight in the making.

Fortunately, Monalisa witnessed the entire sequence of unintended consequences and called, "Time out! Do y'all think this is a game? Making cookies is fun but serious business."

The children froze, looked up, and blinked through the flour covering their faces. Only their eyes remained flour-free. Monalisa moved the bowls out of the way and handed them both sponges, admonishing them to clean up their mess. Then she took over, scooting the children to the bathroom sinks until it was time to roll out the cookie dough.

"Sorry, Miss Monalisa," Joel said when she called the kids back to the kitchen.

Janie added, "What he said."

Monalisa handed them cookie cutters in the shape of bulbs, reindeer, Christmas trees, and stars. "We'll start with the bigger cutters." She showed them how to plan the placement of the cookie cutters. "It's like a puzzle. Figure out how you can get the most cookies out of one rolling. We'll gather the scraps and use the small cutters to make little cookies. That way, the dough doesn't get wasted."

Soon, the delicious smell of baking sugar permeated the house.

"This will make Mom hungry," Janie said, then ran to

Mallory's room. She returned after a bit and said, "You can smell the cookies in her room. That means another scent to help wake Mom.

Monalisa kept a close eye on the cookies. She didn't want a tray of them to burn like they usually did. She was usually alone when baking, and despite the mess, the kids did help prevent her task overload. No cookies were burning this year.

"Later on, can we make Gingerbread people? Those make a really good smell. For Mom."

Monalisa chuckled. "Yes, we can."

CHAPTER TEN: DECK THE TREE

Thursday Afternoon Before Christmas

Sloane entered the kitchen. "Anyone ready for lunch?" The children rubbed their bellies, groaning.

Monalisa winked. "I think they've already eaten."

"Christmas dough bellyaches, eh?" She chuckled when she only heard more groans.

Joel grimaced. "I'm not hungry, Mom."

Janie scowled. "Don't use the f-word, Miss Sloane."

Sloane laughed. "I used the L-word as in *lunch*. It rhymes with bunch."

Joel bellowed, "Don't say it again. It makes me sick."

She smiled and rustled Joel's hair. "Why don't you two go work it off? The tree in the living room won't trim itself."

The children jumped down and ran into the living room where the tree stood waiting in the bay window. Sloane and Monalisa set the kitchen to rights while the cookies finished baking, then joined Seth and the kids.

Monalisa supervised from the couch, delighting them with the stories of the ornaments they hung. "Your dad decorated this sand dollar when he was your age, Joel."

Joel examined it. "Fire! It's a pirate ship with two pirates. One says *Whitt* and the other *Joe*." His gaze filled with awe. "I'm like my dad."

"I see him in you," Seth said. "Decorating these sand dollars was another thing we did together as kids." He held up his ornament with another pirate scene. "We did everything

52

pirate, just like you."

Joel ran to Monalisa's studio, grabbed his ornament, and returned to the tree. "Look at mine. It's kinda like my dad's." He hung it on a bough near Whitt's and smiled. "Like father, like son."

Monalisa brought out cranberries and popcorn for stringing, and the family lent a hand.

Joel complained but quickly found a solution. "I'm just gonna stick to stringing cranberries. My popcorn keeps breaking."

Monalisa looked at his work. "A cranberry garland is pretty, too."

A fire roared in the fireplace, and darkness fell like a curtain outside. Seth put the plug in the outlet, and the Christmas tree lights twinkled brightly, creating a beautiful and awesome picture. They released a collective sigh. Magic was in the air.

Sloane moved close to Seth. He very deliberately dangled a sprig of mistletoe over her head. She turned and accepted his stirring kiss, but two things broke them apart.

One was a strong suggestion from Monalisa. "Oh, for heaven's sake, get a room you two."

The other was an audible sigh coming from the parlor.

Janie gasped. "Did you hear that?"

Everyone rushed to the room to see Mallory's and saw her eyes were opened, looking at the tree.

Janie ran to the bed. "Mom can see the tree. She likes it!" She grabbed Mallory's hand. "Use your words next time, Mom."

Sloane laughed, having said the same thing to Joel at least a million times.

Sloane and Seth exchanged a worried glance and moved closer to the bed. Mal somehow seemed to glow as if she *had* seen the shining tree.

"Doesn't she look better Uncle Joe? I told you so." She turned to her mother. "Keep it up, Mom. You look better every time I see you. Let me tell you about our ornaments. Joel and I made these rad sand dollar snowmen . . ."

Chapter Eleven: How Sweet It Is

Thursday Evening Before Christmas

Sloane looked at Seth after the children announced they had a Christmas project to tend to. Something about a menu. He simply shrugged.

Monalisa smiled at her with a teasing glint in her eyes. "This would be a good time for you two to uh . . . go Christmas shopping. There are some nice shops near the hotel you stayed in last night." She all but added a *hint, hint* to the end of her comment.

"Thanks," Seth said. "Are you sure it's not too much to ask of you after all the baking and decorating?"

Monalisa put her hand on her hips, glaring at him like he was crazy. "I wouldn't suggest it if I thought otherwise. Those longing looks you've been giving Sloane are hot enough to burn her and the house down. Don't think I missed seeing how your eyes are devouring her."

Sloane giggled.

"Well, girlie, don't you laugh. Don't think for a minute that I didn't notice you eye Seth each time he moved a muscle or bent over or stretched or—"

Sloane covered Monalisa's mouth and blushed. Seth, of course, pumped his burly arm like some sort of he-man.

"I don't need any incentive. Come on, Sloane." He grabbed her hand and tugged her to the coat rack. "Time's awastin'." The way his gaze grew heavy-lidded when he looked at her, and the sound of her name on his lips made her melt like a chocolate bar in the summer sun.

"Merry Christmas," Monalisa said, winking. "Oh, by the way, I booked a room for you two at the Sea Glass Hotel again. I know how busy things get before Santa comes. I'll see you in the morning, now, shoo, get outta here before you set the house on fire."

Sloane's face flamed, but Seth took it in stride. They stuck their heads into Monalisa's study to say their goodnights to the kids. The children looked up and covered whatever they were working on.

Seth chuckled. "You two listen to Monalisa, and we'll see you in the morning."

Joel waved and said, "Bye."

Janie looked at her uncle. "What he said."

Sloane threw a look at Seth after closing the door. "What are those kids up to?"

Seth shrugged. "Who knows? Who cares? Let's get outta here while the going's good."

They left the Bradford house, finding falling snow and the slightest breeze greeting them, making the sea air brisk. Sloane couldn't help nearly swooning when she saw his muscles straining the shearling jacket he donned. He filled it out well. She wanted to rip it off him, along with the rest of his clothes, and have her wicked way with his body.

It didn't take long to get to the end of Main Street. With snow gently falling and the town lit up for the holiday, it made the perfect Christmas scene. He noticed a horse hitched to an old-fashioned carriage, stomping in the cold and chafing at the bit. A look-a-like Santa in a car passed them and winked. The driver certainly looked like the epitome of good ole Saint Nick, wearing red suspenders, a Santa hat, and a Swiss-style plaid vest. The kids would be squealing with sheer delight if they were here seeing him.

"You folks up for a romantic ride through Sears Park?" the guy next to the horse called out.

Sloane rubbed her hands together, appearing to glow with excitement. "I'd love to."

Seth took advantage of her proximity and kissed her welcoming lips. She gasped and gave the kiss many promising delights to come.

The man helped Sloane into the carriage. "You picked a good night for a carriage ride." He waved away Seth's offer to pay. "Don't need yer money. This is your lucky night. They'll roll up the sidewalks soon. That means your ride is on me."

Seth shrugged and climbed into the carriage, sitting next to Sloane.

"Snuggle up to your honey, sweetie," the man invited, covering them with a furry blanket, and off they went.

The ride through the wooded park provided a virtual festival of lights. Every tree was illuminated with fairy lights, and the grounds were covered with lighted sculptures of dolphins, lobsters, and whales. The town hadn't skipped the more traditional themes either. The usual toy soldiers, reindeer, snowmen, angels, and even a Polar Express train sprang up like dandelions. Their brilliance made the night magical. The stars shimmered through the falling snow, making the scene look like they were in a snow globe.

"How nice! I love the nautical light sculptures the best. This is heavenly," Sloane sighed. "It's Like being in a Hallmark movie."

Seth chuckled. "I *shore* hope not!" He winked. "See what I did there?"

"Very witty. Very nautical of you." She paused, looking confused. "You have something against Hallmark movies?"

He cleared his throat. "Those shows never come close to coitus, not even coitus interruptus! They don't let the lead characters kiss half the time. It's always interrupted or happens only at the end. They never get to do this." He stroked her jawline gently, running his finger down the length of her platinum locks, tucking the strands behind her ears and out of his way. "And Hallmark never lets the hero do this." He ran his tongue along the shell of her ears, which he knew drove her mad.

The horse must have picked up their vibes, because he snorted and picked up the pace. Sloane shivered, so he snuggled her into the heat of his body, itching to get her clothes off as fast as possible. He couldn't resist stroking her face, her lips, her jawline. He pulled her zippered parka down, kissed the hollow of her throat, and slipped his fingers along a teensy piece of exposed collarbone, learning he had uncovered a previously unknown erogenous zone. In a heartbeat, their romantic Christmas carriage ride seemed to be taking forever.

When they got near the Sea Glass Hotel, Seth asked the driver to drop them off.

The old gent complied. "Ride's not finished, but . . ." With a twinkle in his eye, he added, "Happy to comply. Ho! Ho! Ho! And goodnight."

Seth jumped down as soon as the carriage stopped and turned to give Sloane a hand. "Let me escort you, pretty lady." He helped her dismount and wrapped an arm around her shoulder, moving her forward with an urgency building in his groin.

They entered the inn and retrieved the key to their room, and Seth instantly turned them toward the staircase instead of the bar for a nightcap. Once they reached their room, he used the keycard, hurried them into the room, and got her out of her winterwear as quickly as he could.

She assisted by hauling his jacket off and letting it fall where it might. He kissed her hungrily and lifted her sweater off her shoulders, sweeping her scrap of barely there red lace bra off with it. He kicked off his boots and shrugged out of his shirt and pants quickly so he could watch her do the same. When she tugged down his boxer briefs, his junk jumped up like a jack-in-the-box.

He groaned when she wrapped her fingers along his shaft and caressed his length. He walked her backward to the bed, kissing her, long, hard, urgently plundering her mouth with his tongue while tugging her panties off. Her platinum hair fanned out on the pillow as he lay her down and kissed her until he needed to take a breath. He stared into her eyes as her arms stretched out, dragging him down on her until her nipples met his heaving chest. He bent his head and ever so softly kissed his way around her jawline and down the slim column of her neck, nipping, teasing, playing with her composure. She shuddered and squirmed beneath his onslaught when he captured her delightful breast in his mouth. He grabbed her arms and held them in one hand above her head as he continued driving her crazy with his tongue and lips.

Sloane urged him to plunge inside her, but he did not oblige. No, he continued exchanging his lips for his fingertips as he traced her shivers. He slowly dragged one finger down to her mound, playing with her curls and probing her folds. Her musky scent assailed his senses driving his desire even higher. *Sweet mother of God – this woman drives me crazy.*

He plunged his finger deep into her dripping channel, kissing her lips before moving down her body and using his mouth on her outer folds and inner labia. When he used his tongue to capture her juices, she clawed at his fingers, clearly trying to ease her building pressure arising from his stirring. He wouldn't let her. He brushed her hands away and continued his assault, slipping another finger inside her wet, hot, core. She writhed and cried out. He thrust his fingers in and out of her rhythmically as his tongue toyed with her clit, stroking it gently until she flooded him with her juices.

He paused and looked up. "What? You like this?"

She didn't answer, but her groans spoke volumes. She bucked as she flew apart. Her climax nearly broke his control, but his overwhelming need to please her won out.

He caressed her arms and shoulders, calming her somewhat before kissing along her jawline down and across her collarbone to build her up again. He sucked the tender skin of her neck and then moved on to her breast. Knowing her nipples would be sensitive and need a light touch, he gently flicked his fingers over them ever, then sucked one succulent tip into his mouth. She whimpered as he moved to the other nipple, increasing the pressure a teeny tiny bit. She worked her legs out and encircled his waist with them, pulling him closer until he surrendered to his need with a groan and buried himself deep within her very hot body. It didn't take much before she was screaming another release, and he followed her into ecstasy, spilling everything he had into her.

He collapsed on her, and then shot up. "Oh my God! We didn't use a condom."

She smiled sleepily and purred, "I know."

"I'm so sorry, Sloane."

She rubbed his chest, soothing him somewhat. "Relax. What's done is done. I can deal."

He sat up. "My juju is probably as weak as my bod."

She burst up and smacked his arm. "Knock it off, buddy. Your semen is probably as potent as ever. Chillax."

"I've been half a man since the shark bite."

"Bullshit! You have not. You've been hard as a rock."

"Ask my physical therapist. He's always complaining. Making me do more and harder reps."

Sloane slapped his arm again. "Your leg is healing beautifully. Your therapist even said as much."

"Hmm. He doesn't tell me that. He just pushes me around harder."

She winked. "That's because you are so big and strong and can take the extra workout. A little limp has nothing to do with fertility. I'm fine with it."

He puffed up with her praise. "Maybe we should get married."

She giggled. "You already proposed. I'm still dealing with Whitt, though."

"I can't compete with his ghost."

She yawned. "Grief isn't a one-and-done thing. You don't get over it like a cold."

"We all have ghosts of one kind or another."

"Guess we need a ghostbuster."

"Yeah, but my proposal still stands."

"Yup. Now, let me sleep. We're good. I'm good."

Friday Morning Christmas Eve

The next morning, Seth awoke and found Sloane burrowed into him. *Damn, she feels good.* He ran his fingers up and down the length of her sweet as honey, warm as melted chocolate, skin.

She stirred.

Leaning over her, he stroked her shoulders, arms, and neck. He loved playing with her silver locks and combed his fingers through them.

Sloane pushed her soft as silk ass against his morning wood. "You up, handsome?"

He grinned, and throwing the covers back, he looked. "Oh yeah. For you, I'm always up."

"Mm."

His cock poked at her back, leaving strings of moisture behind. She purred, making him leak even more.

She rolled over and said, "Something happened to your penis. It's wet and hard." She giggled when he took her hand

and guided it to his dick. "I see it's triple in size."

"Do tell."

"What do you think happened to it?"

He grinned and shrugged. "I dunno, but I know what'll fix it and make it return to normal."

"Oh? You better show me in case it ever happens again."

"With that tight, hot, lit body, it'll happen again and again."

She made big eyes and tried to sound all innocent and sincere. "Well, anything I can do about it?"

"I think," he said, positioning her on top of him, "when you sit on it, that should do the trick."

She wiggled over him. "Oh my, it's so big. Will it fit in li'l ol' me?"

"We'll just have to see."

After some minor adjustments, Sloane slid down his rod, enveloping him like a glove. After their romp, she jumped up and headed for the shower, running the water until it was just right. She got in and started soaping her body, and he slipped in behind her, using the suds to caress her body.

She purred. "Shower sex, eh, cowboy?"

She soon turned with soapy hands and explored the contours of his back, arms, and shoulders. She soaped every single square inch of him but stopped when she got to his rod. "Oh, soap won't work here?"

"No? Why not?"

"Because this works better." She rinsed him off with the flexible shower head, then she got down on her knees, played with his sacks, lifted his sex into her mouth, and licked him clean.

"Good God, woman! I'm coming!" He tried to pull away, but she held him firm, sucking him dry. His release trembled through his body, and it took everything in him to keep standing.

"Mm, mm, good." She wiped her mouth and smiled.

He lifted her and said, "Your turn."

She didn't argue. "Be my guest."

After another explosive release, Sloane smiled, thinking of recent events and Seth's worry that he hadn't used a condom. She smiled like the Cheshire Cat. *No worries. No need.* She decided she needed a little something to add to the gift she had already created for him. No*t that I didn't have some divine help with my little package.*

They dressed and went down to breakfast. Sloane's appetite was something else lately, but she managed. After they ate, Seth went to check them out, and she perused the Sea Glass Shoppe and found just what she needed. The pink sea glass whale was the perfect addition to the prettiest baby bottle she had ever seen. She hoped he liked it as much as she did. She couldn't help but feel a niggling chance that he might not. *What then?*

Chapter Twelve: Dinner's On Us

Friday Night Christmas Eve

Janie and Joel were ready to spring their dinner plans. Janie had the vest Joel needed, the tea towel, the tray, Uncle Joe's tie, and most importantly, the menu. She wanted to set the table early, but Aunt Monalisa pointed out that they needed to decorate more sugar cookies, and Joel insisted the gingerbread people needed frosting clothes.

Monalisa had some rules this go-round. "No food fights today. There's too much to do. We have Midnight Mass tonight also."

Joel bounced around the room, pumping his arms. "Operation Parent Wedding is on track."

Janie thought for a minute. "Our goal is to get them married. We'll be a family then. Things are falling into place. I think Mom's better, too. She opened her eyes and squeezed my hand. I think she's waking up."

"All these baking smells must be working. She even sneezed when I spilled pepper under her nose. I swear." He crossed his heart.

Monalisa stopped mixing food coloring into the white vanilla frosting. "You didn't tell me that."

"I didn't wanna get yelled at."

Monalisa smiled at him. "You won't get yelled at. You can tell any of us anything without fear."

Joel looked up, hopeful. "Even if I peppered Ms. Mallory? Some just spilled."

Monalisa nodded. "Even then."

Janie and Joel busied themselves with frosting and clothing cookies, chatting about their creations.

"I made pink and white sea stars," Janie said.

"Look, green Grinch gingerbread man at your service." Joel showed off what he'd done. "And my Superman snowman is way cool."

"I made black boots for gingerbread Santa."

"Show me!"

"My Christmas ornament is half green, half red."

Joel laughed. "It's two-toned."

"I made a rainbow dress for my gingerbread girl."

Monalisa looked at their creations and said, "These are the best-dressed gingerbread family on Cape Cod. While they set, we need to clean up. Your Uncle and Miss. Sloane finished up their Christmas shopping and should be home soon. Why don't you get ready so you can serve your dinner and then we'll go to Mass."

"Okay, yay!" Janie and Joel chorused.

They raced off to complete their plan.

Things took longer than Sloane and Seth expected. Their shower pushed their schedules back, so they arrived home at dusk. As soon as they got their coats off, hung up, and dealt with their packages, the kids ambushed them.

Sloane almost laughed when she saw Joel dressed up like it was Halloween in December, wearing a vest, bow tie, and white shirt and bearing a tea towel on his arm. Janie wore a red jumper and held big cardboard books.

"Good evening, madame and Mr. Seth. We can seat you now. Dinner will be served in our dining room. Walk this way." Joel walked like a penguin, leading them to the room. "I was gonna walk like an Egyptian, like I saw on *YouTube*, but this is more fun."

Sloane smiled at Seth, he shrugged, and they followed Joel into the dining room, walking like penguins, too. The table was set with Christmas paper plates and cups. A potted poinsettia and two lit Christmas candlesticks were arranged between the two settings.

Joel held her seat for her. When she and Seth were seated, he stood between them and said, "I will be your server tonight. Janie, my assistant, will bring your menus. Can I offer you some tea or water?"

Sloane played along. "Water would be nice."

Joel released a sigh. "Good. I don't know how to make tea."

Janie set a big cardboard book, which turned out to be the menus, in front of her and handed another to Seth.

Seth took a look at the menu. "I'll order the Proposal Triangle Toast, please."

"Me too," Sloane added.

"Very good. We serve that with a side of peanut butter and grape jelly, or you can have plain ole butter." His brow creased for a moment. "You can have cinnamon and sugar if you prefer."

"The peanut butter and jelly will be fine," Seth said. "Why is it called Proposal Triangle Toast?"

"Well, sir, most people like our dinner and propose. Maybe you'd like to do that. It's very romantic."

"It certainly is."

Sloane nearly choked on the water Janie had handed her moments earlier.

"Your meal will be ready very soon." Joel gave them a slight bow. "Please enjoy our playlist of Christmas carols while you wait."

The kids left the room giggling.

Sloane turned to Seth, stunned. "Can you believe this? They're setting us up with a romantic dinner."

"Yeah, I feel like proposing."

"Again?"

"Yeah."

"You have a ring this time?"

"I do."

"That's my line. I think you took the words right out of my mouth.

He smiled. "Give me a minute." He left the room a second and returned with a small red velvet box. "I was going to give you this tomorrow."

Sloane leaned over and kissed him. They broke apart when the kids returned.

"It's working, Janie, it's working. They're kissing."

"Sh!" Janie said. "We hope you enjoy your dinner."

Joel ran to the kitchen and returned with two bowls in his hands. "I almost forgot your salads. Well, lettuce and small tomatoes and dressing."

The children left the room with Joel calling, "We'll be back soon with a homemade dessert for you."

Sloane smiled, bemused by what the kids had done. She squeezed Seth's arm. "Don't propose yet. Wait for dessert so the kids can see." She blinked back tears.

"Okay." He leaned in and gave her a quick kiss before they dug into their meals.

Janie and Joel returned with the dessert. Both were practically bursting with excitement. Together, they hummed the Wedding March as they placed the Christmas Gingerbread cookies down. The one for her wore a white frosting veil, and Seth's had a black top hat.

Seth grinned. "You two trying to tell us something?"

They stopped humming simultaneously and looked all innocent.

Joel cleared his throat as he set homemade candy canes on their plates. "Do you need anything else, sir? Do you need a ring? Uh, a refill?

Seth let loose a huge belly laugh. "I just happen to have a ring here."

Joel's mouth widened, forming a huge O, and Janie's eyes grew big.

Janie squealed, "They're doing it! He's proposing. Aunt Monalisa, they're getting married!"

Aunt Monalisa beamed as she stepped out the kitchen door, wiping a tear away with the corner of her apron.

Seth got down on one knee. "This is not quite how I pictured it, but . . . Sloane, will you—"

The grandfather clock in the hall bonged nine times.

"Now hold on you two. Mercy me." Monalisa placed a hand on her heart. "If you don't shake a leg, we'll miss Midnight Mass. We have to leave now. After Mass, Father Nick will be coming over to bestow a Christmas Blessing for Mallory and this household. I wasn't going to tell yet, but Merry Early Christmas. Now, let's get Hank to take over, and we'll pick this all up after Mass."

Joel looked at the clock. "But . . . I'm confused. It's not midnight yet. We have plenty of time."

Janie put her hands on her hips, tapping her foot impatiently. "Don't you know it begins early so you can get a seat? Around here, everyone and their brother and sister go to church on Christmas Eve. There's a sing-along with the Christmas Choir, and we sing Baby Jesus into the world. He's like Cinderella. He has to be home before midnight to help Santa so we get our gifts."

"I never get to stay up that late, and I've never been to church at night. Is what Janie said true, Mom?"

Sloane nodded. "Something like that. There are lots of customs, legends and traditions. Let's go and find out. We better leave if it's that crowded."

"Hold on. Give me a minute." Joel rushed to his room and

quickly returned with an envelope sticking out of his back pocket.

Everyone scrambled, grabbing coats, boots, hats, and gloves, then headed for the car.

Monalisa grabbed Seth's arm before he went out the door. "I'm bushed. It's Hank's shift, but I think I'll stay here with Mallory and Hank. Don't forget to bring Father Nick home with you."

Monalisa gathered the quilt she'd made for Mallory and entered Mallory's room.

Hank smiled and said," She's a bit restless. I'm hoping the lavender will give her some comfort."

"I smell pine."

Hank chuckled. "It's Christmas Eve. I added some cedar, pine, and peppermint just because. I'll give you a minute."

Monalisa cleared her throat. "Hold on a second, help me spread this Christmas quilt over her. I made this when she was born. Did you know she was born on Christmas Day?

Hank chuckled. "Oh yeah, I know. She always thought it was a gyp."

Monalisa clucked. "She's the best Christmas gift this family ever got. Go have a cup of mulled wine or cider while I talk with her."

She caressed Malory's forehead, praying her eyes would open. "Baby girl, I hope you enjoy all the love this quilt holds for you. It's made from generations of Christening gowns and favorite clothes from the family who preceded you. I know you treasure it. Please pull all the healing love and wake up. Janie has had us all talking your ears off. She's done everything she can to get you back with us. It's up to you, my girl, and God."

Monalisa left the room, giving Hank time to follow the

doctor's recent orders. She stood in the doorway and watched as he removed the ventilator mask and replaced it with a cannula.

"Wake up, Sleeping Beauty," he said. "Time for you to take charge and give us our Christmas miracle. The ball's in your court, Miss Mallory. Come claim your birthday gift."

Sloane was happy they had left for St. Joan of Arc Catholic Church when they did. It was a thirty-minute drive when the roads weren't snowy and slick. Thankfully, they were in Seth's four-wheel drive SUV and made the trip safely.

When they walked past St. Joan's statue, shining in her holiday lights, Sloane noticed Janie hesitating when she got near the statue. Janie spent a few moments staring up at St. Joan's face, then she nodded, smiled, and followed the rest of the family into the church.

Sloane slipped into the pew with her makeshift almost family and joined the sing-along. The children sang their hearts out, and Sloane savored the event, feeling both happy and sad, conflicted but certain. Her first Christmas without Whitt was wrought with confusion. Whitt had made her promise to go to Cape Cod to find his friend. Did he somehow know they would fall in love? Then she remembered Monalisa telling her that Whitt always talked about how she and Joe would be *good for each other*. She prayed that what she was doing was what Whitt meant—especially since her heart said it felt right. *Good thing I reserved the right to propose.*

She snapped out of her musing when a man who looked suspiciously like the round-bellied, white-bearded caretaker of the hotel and their carriage driver in the park walked down the center aisle.

The Santa—Priest?—walked to the front and stood behind the altar. He smiled at the congregation and said, "Merry

Almost Christmas, everyone. I know you expected Father Nick, but we exchanged places, and he's at my house in the North Pole. Doesn't matter where home is. God is always present. Let us pray. In the name of the Father . . ."

When the offering basket came around, Joel slipped his note into the basket. The Father took the offerings, raised them, and gave thanks. He held the Eucharistic service and then began distributing Communion. Joel had made his First Communion, so he joined the Communion line and accepted the host.

"Thank you," he said, then quickly corrected himself, "I mean Amen." He followed Janie back to the pew and bowed his head, praying and welcoming his Savior. "Please and thank you. Can I have a family?" He'd bet Janie was praying for her mom.

The Santa priest accepted a slip of paper from an usher. He read it, placed his finger by the side of his nose, and seemed to vanish into thin air. Everything slowed as if time froze, like a glitch in a video game. Then in a blink, everything was normal again, and Father Nick was doing the Communion.

After Father Nick finished dealing with the milling congregation at the end of the Mass, he approached Seth in the church foyer. "I have your address and will drive right over. I have a few items to get first." His eyes twinkled when he turned to him and Janie and winked.

Joel nudged Janie. "Did you see that? He's got to be —"

"Sh! Don't say it. You'll jinx it. Do you want to mess with Christmas magic?"

CHAPTER THIRTEEN: LOOKS LIKE A CHRISTMAS MIRACLE

Sloane's stomach fluttered a bit when the Whitman Bradford family finally got home. It was late, but they had unfinished business to complete. She was somewhat surprised to see Father Nick's red 4x4 had beat them to the house. When they entered the house, all seemed calm and peaceful, yet Sloane sensed a little magic in the air.

Without saying a word, everyone shed their winter wear and crept into Mallory's room, which smelled like Christmas. The small evergreen Christmas tree on the bedside table cast a warm and cheerful glow through the dimly lit room. A fresh pine garland draped across the mantle, adorned with flicker candles, added the perfect touch.

Father Nick looked like Father Christmas with his round jelly belly, full white beard, and long wavy hair. He anointed Mallory's forehead with holy oil in the sign of a cross as he chanted his blessing. "Daughter of God, member of His Holy Church, I grant you Christ's peace. May this oil and holy water bring you healing, health, and joy. I anoint, bless, and bring you to His peace. Your church family and your heavenly family bid you well. May you celebrate Christ's birth and see many more. In Jesus's name, amen." His gaze swept over everyone else in the room. "Dear family, I enjoin you to share with Mallory as you celebrate the joy of Christmas. Bless this house and all who dwell within. The sacrament of Healing and Reconciliation is hereby complete. I bid you goodnight and a Merry Christmas."

Sloane felt a lightness in her heart. Somehow, the blessing was not at all a sad event. No, to the contrary, it felt warm and hopeful, not pious and dreadful.

Father Nick paused by Joel and Janie as he headed out of the room. He winked, then whispered, "Believe. Ho, ho, ho, Merry Christmas. Never stop believing."

The family spent time with Mal, sharing their day, then drifted into the living room, leaving Mallory's door wide open and gathering near the tree. Joel and Janie sat on the floor, and Sloane and Monalisa sat on the couch.

Seth disappeared, but soon returned, approaching Sloane and getting down on one knee. He cleared his throat and said, "Now . . . Where was I?"

"You were gonna ask Mom the big question," Joel encouraged.

Seth winked. "Was I?"

"Yes!" Joel and Janie yelled in unison.

Seth grinned. "I just happen to have a ring right here." He pulled a beautiful platinum diamond and pearl ring out of his pocket.

Joel bounced in his seat and clapped his hands. "It matches your hair, Mom! It's fire."

"Dope!" Janie added and turned to Monalisa with rounded eyes. "He's doing it, Aunt Monalisa! He's proposing. They're getting married!"

"Now hold on a minute." Aunt Monalisa beamed as she wiped a tear away with a hanky. "It's not over yet."

Seth chuckled and looked into Sloane's eyes. "This is not quite how I pictured doing this, but . . . Sloane, will you do me the honor of marrying me? I know I'm no longer the man I was. I'm just a half-broken man, but I'm offering my whole heart. I can't offer you a family and give you another child — there's been nerve damage — but I'll give you all I have. Marry me."

"Stop. Just stop, please. You think you can't give me a family, but I can give you one. I'm the one who should propose. I wasn't going to give you your gift tonight, but it's time." Sloane bent down and retrieved a gift bag. "Open this."

He opened the bag. A huge smile spread across his face. "Does this mean what I think it does?" He held up a baby bottle with a pink whale.

Sloane nodded. "I can give you a family of Joel and baby Star if that's what you want. I'm having a baby girl. I hope you'll say yes and marry the three of us?"

"Huh? This is too good to be true. Really? How? When? It wasn't that long ago that we . . ."

"The usual way. Last summer. Remember?"

"Boy, do I!"

Something fell in the parlor. Monitors started beeping loudly and every piece of machinery buzzed or chimed. They rushed to see what caused the racket as the grandfather clock bonged twelve times.

Mallory's eyes were wide open as she stared at Seth and managed to croak, "Say yes, bro."

Pandemonium broke out.

Monalisa beamed. "Mercy me! What a night! It's a Christmas miracle!"

Joel pumped his arms and jumped around. "See? I told you so. We got everything we wanted this Christmas."

"It's the best Christmas Ever!" Janie rushed into her mother's arms, telling her at the top of her lungs that Uncle Joe was getting married.

Mallory's eyes blinked and she cupped Janie's face. "I know, baby girl. I heard every word. You guys talked my ears off."

Sloane smiled at Seth.

He picked her up and twirled around as he kissed her

passionately, then whispered. "My answer is yes."
  Sloane whooped. "Yep. The best Christmas ever."

The End

OTHER BOOKS BY KATHY KALMAR

The Beach Series

Beyond the Beach Book One
Beyond the Beach Book Two
Beyond the Beach Book Three
Beyond the Beach Book Four
Beyond the Beach Book Five
Back to the Beach Book One
Back to the Beach Book Two
Promises on the Beach

The Mountain Series

Mountain Hot
Mountain Christmas
Mountain Skye Prequel to the Weather Girls
Mountain Kiss
Mountain Joy
Mountain Promises
Mountain Holly
Mountain Silver
Mountain Mistletoe
Mountain Bred
Mountain Led
Mountain Wed
Mountain Hookup
Mountain Fever

Mountain Due
Mountain Bachelor
Mountain Match

The Cape Cod Series

Cape Cod Promise
Cape Cod Connection
Cape Cod Christmas

About the Author

Kathy Kalmar, born in Detroit, Michigan, lives with Larry, her husband of forty-plus decades. Lately, she feels her life has recovered from the bad country song-like life because her Smoky Mountain Tops Round House is rebuilt from the 2016 Chimney Tops II Wildfire in which she is writing her next book in her Writing Room. Her current residence is enlarged by four feet with the addition of their new puppy. She loves to read and write contemporary romance novels. Meanwhile, she remains fond of hot tubbing, chocolate, and sipping wine and mai tais and moonshine whether at home, Waikiki, Cape Cod, or Tennessee. Y'all come back, hear?

Contact Kathy at KathyKalmar.com